j-afrikah presents

PAINTING FROM THE HEART
The story of Iman

Jeremy A.R Davis

A J-AFRIKAH PRODUCTION

Bridgetown, Barbados

jeremyd4@gmail.com

Copyright © 2013 Jeremy Davis

ISBN: **978-1490988658**

For:

My mother- The greatest woman in the world!

Jewel- The second greatest woman in the world, and best friend a brother could have.

My father- I feel you man.

I dedicate this one to those who can't sleep at night for their poetry keeps them awake and tormented.

I acknowledge-
 Life, love, laughter and hope

And rebuke-
Pain, sickness, sadness, death and disease.

FROM THE AUTHOR

Here's something I thought you'd enjoy!

I feel like I sped through my first book... forgive me! *My Mother's Son*, even though well received and reviewed was, to be honest, an experiment. I've always been terrified of an early death without ever having the opportunity to get to call myself a published writer, and so what you have there is a rushed project from an impatient child. I've grown! I've travelled extensively, taught, spoken to young people about patience and goals, learned a lot in the process, matured ... a bit. I know better. I've developed my craft and so I write better! Essentially- this is the book you should've read first and I suppose that this is the book that I should have written first.

In a way, I feel this is the book I've always been trying to write. It's always been my raison d'être to pen words that would not only entertain but educate and inspire. My goal, quite frankly, is to move you to tears. My hope is to make you fall in love with me every line you read. I want you to be touched by my characters and characteristics. I'll admit, I've always considered myself a bit of an 'Urban Philosopher', if you will, and I'm blessed that throughout my life so far, I've been relatively accepted as such.

This is another of my proverbial 'brainchild'.

So from my heart to yours, I do hope you enjoy this bit of me.

With Love,

Jeremy A.R Davis (J-Afrikah)

SHORT STORY

SHORT STORY

Painting from the Heart (Pt. 1): IMAN

Painting from the Heart is a classic Caribbean novelette with all the novelties of a fresh 21st century, piece of Caribbean literature. It is about an artist's desperate search for love and his inability to find it.

Iman is a traveled and cultured Barbadian. He is a Rasta! He seems to have everything he could want but is unsatisfied. This book takes the reader through a portion of his life and subsequent migration from Barbados to the UK. It takes you from sadness to sadness to disappointment to glorious triumph and joy to unfortunate sadness again-c'est la vie. It is a rollercoaster of emotions that will sweep the most hard-heartened off their feet.

Painting from the Heart shows us what is really important in life, and it shows us that when we take things like love and life for granted there are those who lack these things and envy us. To me this is ironic.

BARBADOS

Chapter I

Masterfully stroking his small brush on the huge wall in anticipation of the enormous task that was set before him, he painted…and smiled; this wall was to serve as a canvas.

Iman was busy creating another one of his famed and acclaimed murals. This one, like the others, would serve as a reminder, beyond his death, proving to the future that he had actually existed on this earth at a time before. With his pieces of priceless creations each bearing chippings of his soul strategically spread out around the universe, no one could doubt his descendants of his greatness.

It was clear to see by passers-by, passing by with awe in their eyes, the extent of commitment that Iman had invested in his work. Resting his own eyes gently on the nose of his freshly painted Nubian Princess, one character in his creation, he sifted through his work for an imperfection that he could repaint or fix; Iman was a perfectionist. Head slightly tilted to the right side, rocking back and forth to the sweet

Barbadian calypso sounds of *Boots* by the Mighty Gabby in his headphones, he was drawing inspiration garnered from a life of good intentions, bad habits and a rollercoaster of emotions and expressions that lived in a mind wearied from a lifetime of experience.

Iman skips back and forth on his creation; a 50-foot wide tribute to the private school that he attended during his early teenage years, remembering how he skipped back and forth from the principal's office within these compounds, what now seemed like ages ago. Reminiscing on the good old days of his life made him smile some more smiles and he slowly becomes nostalgic. A self acclaimed poet, he sketches the words to a new poem into his mind:

Verse I

I care not for politics, I do not wish for fame

But how I long to breathe the life that I feel within my veins.

My hands, shaking though they are, don't hope to hold a prize,

But someday, and someday soon, the world will know my name.

His intentions were simple: to mark each phase of his life, every stop he has made; like cavemen drew stick figures to tell their stories, these murals were going to be Iman's autobiography.

Iman stops his movements, almost suddenly, and taps his temple as he tries to soothe his overworking brain from the overload of activity that was taking place on the inside; this is his happy place. Tapping his head, looking at the masterpiece, it was like reading an old diary.

Since his childhood, one of the few things that ever appeased him was art.

"Before, during, and...post during Imanism." Iman cracks a giggle to himself. "What does that mean?"

"I love the smell of paint bleeding off a canvas, as the sun dries my picture." He whispers to himself. Closing his eyes and following his sentence with a deep 'breathe in' to confirm his appreciation for this random potpourri mixture of scents and smooth sounds with the unique feel of the Barbadian afternoon warmth.

"This is where I man lives." Iman stretches his THIS, his I, and his LIVES.

'Real Rastafari style'.

He subconsciously tries to convince himself that the locks on his head mean more than just a monthly visit to the salon and a hundred dollar bill to keep his roots tight. His extended roots were to be symbols of a divine intervention; his reincarnation as a black man and his timely rebirth as a true African. Iman tugs his locks in a bunch. Usually when he does this, he thinks one thing: Black men must pull at their roots to see how much histry comes out. Histry has always been a major part of Iman's life.

Staring at the oil dripping from his brush he wished for an escape. If he could only paint himself in there with his characters, he thought. He did not realize that all these characters were just extensions, rather than inventions, of who he was, of who he has been through the years. So, perhaps he was. Perhaps he was painting himself into the huge brick wall that stood, giant above him. Maybe, he thought, as he stroked, his immortal soul seeped out of his body in some transcendent way and dove into his paintings… the fantasist that he was.

"Iman!"

"Yeahh mamma!"

Iman can almost feel himself mouthing his words in hope that this memory does not abscond itself, disappearing into just wisps of air as the others. Memories do that sometimes. Teasing the senses, tickling the 'wishes' and making you yearn to go back. A great man once said 'memories don't die like people do.' They live long after you, replacing you, and for many, is all that remains after all the material things are desiccated. Some men say that even after a person is dead, he lives on in the minds and hearts of those who knew him. Probably, this is what Iman was intending: to engrave himself in the minds and hearts of all who viewed his art thus expanding his spiritual network.

Iman's mind wandered back to the year he discovered his passion and his love for art. Immediately, he is immobilized by the vividness of this particular 'dream'.

"Iman where yuh deh boy?"

Mamma shouts to Iman

"Ah in de yard widde dog ma" Iman shouts back immediately, hoping though, that he is not called away from his brown and brindle pot hound, Bruno, that he was drawing in the middle pages of his school Mathematics notebook. Bruno looked so content, as he dug inanely into the core of the banana tree.

"Stop playing wid di foolish dog and come inside and wash up for yuh supper NOW Iman."

Coming from humble origins, Iman seems to always find joy in the simple things that life has to offer. Like playing with the dog, digging holes in the backyard and of course, just listening to the rushing sound of the ocean as her waves snatched the air away into her deep, unfathomable blue. That was his favorite pastime. There is something about the beach that makes all life seem lively. Perhaps, just the mere fact that she is never stagnant and keeps constantly moving. Iman was aesthetic, philosophical, for a country boy.

Back then, every day at around 6 a.m., Iman would wake up and without even brushing his teeth, washing his face or eating anything, rush to the ocean, which was literally a stone's throw from his wooden two-bedroom home. The same home that his great grandfather had built, his grandfather had refurbished and he was destined to do some good to maintain.

"Iman, dey got so much histry here in dis hay property yuh know." He remembers paps telling him as they sat for evening tea once or one too many times.

"Histry grandpap. Wuh you mean by histry?"

Saying that Iman wasn't the brightest fella was, no doubt, an understatement. In fact, he was almost ten and still didn't know how to say his times tables straight, but boy could he draw up a storm.

When anything that needed to be captured in the community, they called in Iman; cameras were scarce and Iman was the neighborhood Picasso. By the time he was twelve, he had already painted paintings for even the Principal at his school. But that was it and all the glory ended there. Iman wanted to, but he could see no future in painting.

The way that he was made to see his future had nothing to do with art. He, more than likely, was to end up working on his grandfather's farm, or, if he studied hard enough, get to run the shop for mama. So this whole school thing was a load of crap. And painting...

To Iman, painting was life, the reason why he breathed, but to mamma, painting was child's play. She couldn't understand the value of the aesthetic and so she tried to stifle his passion. Still, every chance Iman got, he rushed back to his first love, quenching his undying thirst for her peace. That was why Iman loved to go to the beach. She gave him an excuse to be with his lover, so Iman loved to paint her. Her sand, like billions of little specky smiley faces welcomed him to the warm blue that was the water. The sun, rising over the horizon, could be likened to his love which was constantly rising and rising for the art although never to set. There was a lot that he had in common with the serenity of the beach and just like the ocean he wanted to see his life constantly moving... away from the poverty stricken village; away from the little shack shack in the country to one of those big mansions out by the big hotels where the tourists stay in St. Lawrence Gap. See, there were no confusing metaphors to understand about that, just real dreams from a real boy.

Some days, Iman would take a walk to the beach and search for new things that he could claim he discovered. He was always finding new things to paint on the beach and at the same time, he was finding himself as well. From shells shaped like diamonds to the sunsets setting over the horizon or just painting the foaming water as it beat incessantly off the rocks. There was always something to paint or draw and Iman vowed that as long as his two eyes could see, and he was blessed enough to have his hands still functioning, he would paint.

"A real man does work in de soil" Mamma always said, enunciating as much as she could have, never having even graduated from high school. "They ain goh no future in dis painting ting, Iman."

Iman had his life cut out for him already, both what he wanted it to be like and what it was going to be like regardless, so he didn't bother study nothing bout no 'histry' because histry hardly fit into any of his life plans.

Iman waited to see whether paps would explain what he was talking about.

"Boy, yuh wudda feel dat we's don't sen you school bout hay… I telling you histry, you telling me…" Paps says with a giggle. "I ain't know whuh dey's be teaching wunna yung boys nowadays anyway."

Iman smiles.

"Iman, this was one O de' first free pieces of land dat we black people had here in Barbados. My father lived here and I, who's you granfadda live in hay too. If these walls coulda talk, rite I," his grandfather never took the time to spell out the two syllables in his name and thought that calling him I would suffice, "dey wudda tell you tings that you never did wan ta even know did going on in this world man. Dem hear all kinds ah ting."

Iman lived with his mother Debra, and his grandfather George, in a small village community in St. James.

His mother, a beautiful mulatto woman, was mixed from her mother's side of the family. Her mother, granpap's wife who had passed away ever since mamma was a girl, had some white in her so mamma's hair was nice and long and it had bounce in it, while his hair looked a lot like granpap's hair, and was always knotty and tangled. Mamma had hazel eyes and was the kind of woman that would make a man say 'mercy lawd' every time she passed by. Iman knew that for sure because that was all the construction workers that worked nearby on the National Housing Council projects used to say when they passed the house on the way to work on mornings.

Mamma used to always sing the old Bajan folksong 'Every time I pass, they pull at me.' Mamma was almost perfect. She was a fine shaped woman with a broad pearly white smile. She worked one of two odd jobs at any given time, one as a maid for Ms. Caukley, the English woman, and one as a babysitter for Ms. Bakden, but she always spent her extra time at the family store; these things, just to make ends meet. It seemed to Iman, when he was growing up, that his mother was always working for a white woman with a funny name. Sometimes, I would try to draw how he saw mamma's bosspeople looking after just catching a glimpse of them dropping her home in their big cars or hearing how mamma described them. Almost all the time, they were caricatures with funny shaped noses, straight thin hair and minute breasts that seemed barely enough to breastfeed an infant protruding from their expensive looking blouses. They had flat bellies, and of course...no boxy at all. Iman always got a laugh from hearing mamma talking about her bosspeople.

Hearing the impressions that she would do in their voices tickled him to death. Mamma should have been an actress; she's so good with accents and doing things on those soap shows. In secondary school, her classmates would always cast her as one of the lead parts because they said that she could capture the emotions and "portray the characters most vividly" and they voted her the most likely to be on Days of our Lives. Iman thinks to himself that in a fair and ideal world, or probably a different dimension, mamma would be a professional actress working in Hollywood, making a cazillion dollars. But in this reality, mamma is a day worker who got pregnant at 16 and had to leave school when her boyfriend's mother found out that "he pregnant a girl" and sent for him from oversees.

"Mamma, do Ms. Caukley in the bathroom when she see de good job that you do pun de winduhs."

Granpap was an older man. Middle aged. His skin was burnt darker than it used to be because he toiled in the sun every day since he was thirteen. His hands were hard and clamp from grinding clay days in and days out. His fingernails were discolored. They were stained by their mixing with the seeds of fruits and vegetables and them dipping in fertilizers. However, paps was surprisingly not grumpy like other oldies. He was always joyful, whistling or humming tunes, either an old Negro Spiritual, or something he'd heard on the radio. Whenever asked about what he was singing or humming, his answers would amuse those who questioned him.

"Dat dey?" He would intrigue, especially foreigners at the market who liked his deep country accent, "is a old Slave chune my yute. Wunna wuddunt know nuttin about dat "

Or…

"My fren, you don't know dat? Dat is Lil' Richie"

Unlike old people in the area, Granpap was neither deeply rooted in religiosities, nor did he see himself as innately spiritual. In fact, the only time church saw paps was on Easter and Christmas. And that was on a good year. One could speculate that he was so content with how he lived his life that, he was not making any last minute dash efforts to be given entry into heaven. And the truth is, Paps was a good man. He always was. He was the kind of man that people liked to be around. He had an aura that attracted all kinds of people to his personality. Many of whom were high profile people that frequented his market stalls sometimes leaving huge tips although Paps told them that they didn't have to.

Iman's grandmother died soon after his mother was born so all that Iman knew about her was the little that granpap had told him in his stories. Mamma remembered nothing. Granpap lived his whole life in these stories and maintained that he only loved one woman since his teenage years. They were high school sweethearts, paps and gran, and out of their union came only one child, mamma, and mamma only had one child, Iman, and Iman's father had deserted him, so all they really had was each other.

Granpap would never have his household depressed though, thinking about all the negatives, and he made it his duty to always revive them when things were dull. He would say "I remember when…" and those were one of the ways you knew to come and sit down because a story was brewing. Iman always wondered to himself if someday he would be like pap, remembering ancient times and living in them. Iman bet that in Granpap's mind, he wished he were still young.

They say that when an old man dies, it's like a library has burned down. When Iman and Mamma came home from Pap's funeral, they sat in the same spots that they used to sit in during pap's stories and wondered what would happen now. Who would keep them entertained now that Paps was gone?

"I guess Paps was tired and lonely, and missed gran, and wanted to see her." Iman told mamma to comfort her. From that day on, Iman would be forced to be man of the house. Iman would have to work harder on the farm, or they would have to sell parts of it to pay the bills.

In Iman's home, there was always little to eat, and there was always water dripping on their heads when it rained, but it was all right; because this was their peace. Their happy place. Within these creaky walls, there was joy. And even though they were poor beyond imagination, and their home wasn't a castle, at least they had each other... and now Paps was gone!

Iman is snatched out of his reverie and awakened by the whizzing past of ZR115 banging the new Lil' Rick song that was to be big for Crop

Over. He could see clearly through the windows the girls who's heads squished against each other's as they sat down on the overly excited teenage boys, no doubt because of the conductor's attempt to stuff double the amount of passengers into his booming van. How many people can fit into a Bajan ZR anyway?

"Oh gosh, must be that time of day again."
Iman looks at his watch and realizes the time.

"Cheese on Bread! Three O' Clock already." Iman hated to be out on the street when school let out.

"These young children have no behavior nowadays" Iman thinks to himself. "I remember when…" Iman stops himself and smiles.

Iman steps back from his painting, squinting, hoping to catch a bigger and better picture of what his masterpiece was beginning to look like. He walks cautiously as he crosses the street and as he gets, finally, unharmed, to the other side he turns slowly to see his, still unfinished, product that he was sure was going to be another 'off the chain' production. Iman marvels at the patchy piece and feels a sense of pride as he watches his creation and feels it coming to life.

"Nice!"

Chapter II

Walking unhurriedly up his porch and toward the glass doors that he had just recently gotten installed, Iman recaps the day's proceedings, wondering why he always gets so involved in his work that he never notices anything else. Since he began painting the mural, he missed lunch almost every single day. He smirks and his head is thrown back slightly as he nods his head pitifully making a clicking noise with his tongue on the roof of his mouth. As he walks into the house, he presses the button under the light switch that closed the gate at the beginning of the long driveway that he had just driven up with his Lincoln Navigator and reaches into his pocket searching for the last stick of Bubalicious gum… his favorite! Iman shoved the sweet chewy goodness into his mouth as he plops down on the couch in the lounge. He takes the remote and sets the CD surround sound player and beautiful BOSE system speakers on extremely loud, and cranks out some conscious music.

He turns to the right and, with a lighter ignites five sticks of incense in a vase. Clouds of smoke begin dancing to beats of *Positive Vibrations*. The passivity of his spirit is enhanced by the aroma in the air and the consciousness of the music. Iman chews, sniffs and vibes' his way into peace as one track gives way to another and another.

This house had come a far way from a leaky roof, a wooden info structure and malfunctioning windows with a huge lot of barely used farmland. It had come a long way from not having anything in the cupboards to the cupboards always being filled to the brim. This house withstood floods in the area, hurricanes, numerous burglary attempts, drive-by shootouts, malicious vandalism, and much more. If this were a bad country, one would understand but Barbados is too beautiful for all this crap to be happening, according to Iman, but then again, Barbados is going to the dogs.

Despite all that, Iman could feel the love as the memories moved him gently through the halls and rooms that were once many square feet smaller. Or perhaps it was the high that he was still enjoying but Iman felt at peace. This place, despite the loss of two key elements, and all the histry that it had endured, was still Iman's castle. It was his home because his heart was there…and if only these walls could talk.

"Mama, I home."

Iman remembers storming into this house when he was a boy…

and he inhales deeply. A new smell is birthed in the air and overpowers

the vanilla air freshener that was used to scent the house. Well this is not a

new smell. This is the smell of that fried chicken and macaroni pie

blending together in a perfect harmony. The same exact smell he used to

smell every Sunday when he came in from the beach only to find mamma

and paps already seated on the table, waiting for him to join them. This

time, sadly, as he opened his eyes, meal blessings hadn't just concluded,

and once again he was standing solitary in his newly renovated fortress

which was now anything but just a homely 'shack'. Completely beyond his

control, Iman realizes that his visions are getting clearer and clearer.

He moves to the den and feels an overpowering urge to drink.

Reluctantly, he pours himself a hot Johnny Walker Scotch from the liquor

cabinet and forces it down…straight. As the alcohol burns, going down

Iman's chest, he enjoys a moment of quiet from his deafening memories

that were screaming for an intrapersonal interaction.

Iman looks around and a sense of accomplishment and extreme

well being overcomes him as he acknowledges his acquirements. He gets

flashbacks as he passes the family room and thinks to himself "This castle

not a Shack Shack no more. If only mamma could see her boy now."

Iman stares at the portrait of his grandfather hanging next to a portrait of his mother's, and a single teardrop rolls from his eye and disappears on his slightly bearded face while at the same time moving a lock from his face and overcoming his pain with a forced smile to maintain himself.

He whispers,

"Yeah paps… now I live in hay too. Now I live in hay too."

Iman walks around the fully modernized three bedroom- two bathroom house with pool, overlooking his lawn space, with an impeccable view of the ocean, all gated and all he could think about was mamma, pap and Bruno. Iman never again saw a family like the one he knew growing up.

Iman looks back and realizes, at that moment, that in this world, he is completely alone and besides his art with which he now spends hours with, he has no one to share his successes with. No love to laugh with. No daughters or sons to tell stories about his past to. Not even a dog that he could go outside and pet until it was time to wash up for supper. Iman began to wonder if at the tender age of 37, his life was over.

He thinks to himself that the saddest part of the whole darn thing was that he had spread no seed, so he had no one to carry on his name; this legacy that he had always spoken of leaving.

Iman sits down on the white lazy boy leather couch in the family room that he'd bought himself, from Persia, and taps his temple. Kicking his legs up on the coffee table, he stares into the emptiness that he called his space and he scribes in his mental notepad:

Verse II

I do not fain perfection; I know I'm just a man

But how I long to make a change and stand for what I can.

My hands, Shacking though they are, don't hope to hold a prize

But still someday, and someday soon, the world will say: Oh what

a man.

Rising slowly, and feeling like he had found a semi solution for his problems, Iman skips to the garage and opens the gateway. After throwing on his jacket, unbuttoned, and his helmet, resting on the top of his head, Iman sticks the key in his bike and pushes the royal blue Kawasaki ZX12R towards the gate. He needed to ride something with body and soul, but something that would still would make him feel like a kid again. The bike always did such a good job.

-*Vbrooom...* The sweet melodious sound of horses waking up to taste the asphalt on a warm summer's evening. Iman kicks away the stand and balances as the engine rattles underneath him sending vibrations through his bum. He listens as the spirit of this ZX12R mutters to him. He knows this language well; he's heard this sound before and at times, when he thought he was alone, he'd spoken back. It is the sound of a fulfilling happiness, there's something about riding a motorcycle that would make any man forget all his troubles…if just for a moment. And they say money can't buy happiness. Iman can remember exactly how much this moment of happiness costs. In fact, he saved the pay slip for his taxes.

Iman pulls away from his fort-like compound with a bellowing cloud of smoke and the sound of tires screeching below a heavy bike engine. He feels the wind threatening to tear away at the flaps of his leather jacket as he speeds out of the main gateway onto the main street. Having Iman had missed lunch combined with the fact that the spirit of the house had been rather unfair to his feelings, Iman decides that he would eat out today…again.

Whenever Iman felt depressed, he could always find comfort at Tyrone's Deli and Bar. The way they did the chicken over there was just like mamma did hers back in the day and 'the feel' of that little family restaurant in Jackson is lovely. It's so Fengshui, just like those cultured white people say in the UK. Iman always ended up forgetting most of his troubles by the time he got there, if not before.

Nowadays, the beach was beginning to take second place as a mediator between Iman and his sanity to Tyrone's, and Iman was cool with that, just as long as Tyrone had some of those sweet chicken tenders for him, everything was all good with the world.

As Iman climbed up the stairs to the family restaurant, he could hear the sound of the T.V working full time in the background. It was cricket season. Naturally, the sounds of both joy and pain could be heard at different times in various high pitched anxious tones. They say cricket is the one sport that joins people together as much as it drifts them apart, especially in the Caribbean. Iman agrees completely, which is why he refuses to sit and watch, not only cricket, but any sporting activity. Iman never was a sports lover anyway. As a child, he'd prefer to sit inside talking to girls and playing house, rather than being outside, playing ball; never the 'run up and down' type of kid.

Iman moves slowly as he opens the door. The air condition blasts countless degrees of cool recycled air into his face. A lovely release from the humid Caribbean environment that embraced him just seconds earlier.

"Tyrone! You inside hay? Tyrone where my chicken is? I hope you ain't sell out all my tenders or I gine gawh lick down sumbody in hay." Iman says, smiling.

Tyrone is an extremely friendly guy and Iman could never help but treat him as well as he sees him treat others.

"Of course not. You know I would never do that." Tyrone laughs back.

Tyrone is the type of chef that goes all out for his customers. They are more like his friends than patrons. If he doesn't have what you ordered, he would go out of his way to get it for you. And if per chance, he still couldn't secure you your order he would promise you that tomorrow, if you came, your order would be waiting, and rest assure when you came back you would have your ideal meal, and with all the fixings that you would expect. Perhaps, it was just that Tyrone was a superb businessman, but Iman liked to think that Tyrone was naturally a nice man and he had taken a real liking to him. These days, Iman would take any love that anyone was dishing out. God knows he craved it.

Because there were so many people at Tyrone's, cricket season and all, and Iman really didn't feel like being involved with crowds, he decided to take his crispy tenders to go. He would take this as a sign; as an opportunity to go back to his first first-love and spend some quality time with her; it'd been a while since he last basked in her presence.

As Iman rode, he could hear remnants of evening breeze through his helmet calling his name, and the setting sun produced a dimming light that was all too euphoric; perhaps a little orgasmic even in a weird sort of

way. Iman pulled up slowly, and parked close to the sand. Peace.

Chapter III

Right as he was getting ready to enjoy his meal- crispy chicken tenders- he looks around and realizes that there are many more couples congregated on the beach than he had expected.

His eyes wandered towards a rather mature couple walking towards the beach bar and grill, hand in hand and barefooted carrying shoes in the available hands. Iman had underestimated this beautiful island in the sun…Barbados. Since the sun set so beautifully in Barbados, couples often come to the beach together after work, to recap on their day and to take advantage of the romantic environment that is. Or just to hold hands and stroll along the shore, smiling.

Iman begins to feel the loneliness creep up on his being once more like it was trying to steal away his mortality. He wished that he had stayed at Tyrone's. It would have been much better for him to sulk in the corner there, listening to the roars and whistles of cricket fans than to have to endure this plethora of romantic relationships teasing his desire for companionship.

Iman's appetite for food is compromised by the sensation of incompleteness and he violently tosses the Styrofoam container containing his lunch and supper and perhaps even his breakfast for tomorrow on the sand. Iman barely ate and as a lone tear manifests itself on his face he knows what he has to do.

"Note to self- when you eat this few amount of times per day, you can't afford to lose your appetite." Iman passes his hand through his head from the back to the front right side, stopping to tap on his temple...Iman style.

"Another moment in the incredible presence of mine own company. Lovely."

He sits on the sand. Facing the consuming ocean with its billions of smiley faces as sands they're no longer smiling. Staring hopelessly at him they're each searching for something. No! Today was different. The sand specks, his friends, did not recognize him and he feels like a stranger among his own friends. With his eyes following the lovers' trails, he thinks.

Pairs and pairs of footprints in the sand; what is it to have someone walk by your side?

Men argue that knowing that someone has your back is the greatest feeling that there is; the best and truest ecstasy; real harmony. The highest highs exist as you're staring aimlessly eyes that stare aimlessly back into yours, because then, and perhaps only then, you feel the endless peace that is. This, they say, that is men that say what they say, is true happiness. Happiness that not even money could buy and not even prestige could inherit. Women agree!

Iman exhales deeply, sighing, as an expression of total and complete dissatisfaction of his life; he gets up and moves slowly towards the sea, rolling up his pants as he approaches the waves.

"God, you know what you was doing dey when you gave Eve to Adam fuh trute yuh." Iman stops ten toes shy of where the water meets the sand, and he tries to think of how Adam must have subsequently felt after God hooked him up with Eve. His satirical mind envisions an Adam that did cartwheels and handstands, not being able to stop kissing God's hands as he beheld Eve's grace. Just like an orphan boy who just received his first toy.

As he moves, tip toeing into the water… he feels the cool Caribbean saltwater on his ankle and knees as the lower half of his pants dampens by the splashing waves. This is where it's at for Iman.

"I'm back baby!" He stoops down closer extending his hand into the water. "How've you been? I missed you a lot sweetheart!" Iman silently talks to this huge body of water like it's a long lost lover sitting down for a more intimate encounter. But she was…his first lover; perhaps, his only true lover, in some people's opinion of what truth is, and other people's opinion of what love is. So, as Iman's toes kissed the sands he walked in, his body basked in the warm embrace of Barbados. A smiling, flirting Barbados; at forty something after independence and she was still… beautiful. She was remarkable.

****

Iman climbs onto his ZX12R, adjusts his helmet, and zooms off Lovers' Spot. Wondering, as he accelerated quickly from gear to gear, how come he never found love in his many travels; why has he never felt the warmth of a heartfelt kiss or the joy of a genuine handhold. Thus, the things that Iman found to be significant stood to be the things that evaded him.

His life, devoted to passion; Iman found it strange that a man whose life was dedicated to beauty never embraced a splendor he could call his own. There were many lovers. Flings in Brazil; romantic encounters with businessmen's wives; tourist honeymooners he stole in Jamaica; and vacationers who liked his work and his style enough to sleep with him, but how many of these could he say was real? None proved long-lasting. This is what Iman searched for: a woman that he could share pillow talk with, after and even before the four or five hour sessions of making love. Iman began to think that he was tired of just the hard-core physical attraction of a relationship, he wanted the soft, mushy stuff that came along with 'it' too.

Iman thinks back and remembers Thelma, the museum curator in Trinidad, with the hair of a goddess. She was the one who got him into early 18th century artifacts. He would go look for this princess every weekend when he was at UWI in St. Augustine. He was nineteen, probably twenty, that time, but the passion that they shared was unbelievable; way beyond his years.

There was also Amanda from Antigua, and beautiful Beth, the Brazilian bombshell. These were the three women that Iman was inextricably linked to for extensive periods of time…sexually. There might have been others, but none as important as these.

He didn't call them girlfriends; he called them 'Beneficial Pit Stops'. Beth was his best 'thing' though. She kissed, and his lips felt like they were they were kissing the lips of an angel. And when she made love to him, it was like all heaven stopped to breathe contentment on his mediocre life. His heart skips beats as he imagines what his life could have been; with a wife, kids…a family; perpetual happiness. A smile rips across his face as he envisions coming home after work to his kids sitting in the family room waiting for him. He imagines telling them stories and throwing in some 'histry' to remind his family of their rich ancestry and then his vision disappears as Iman's existing life flashes before his face…Reality in its most disgusting form. There were no kids, no wife, and no family rooms, just a fully furnished yet empty house and a lonely, approaching middle-aged man. Was this his crisis?

Iman remembers Beth, leaving as quickly as she came and taking with her all the joys that he was to eventually feel. They say that you never miss a good thing till its gone, like when the well has run dry, it is only then you get thirsty, or something like that, but fortunately for Iman, they also say that when one door is closed, God opens another one. "The sad thing is" Iman says to himself, "that since I am not really a religious person or deeply rooted in this church thing, I wonder if he's going to open up doors for me too."

So if only he had known; if only he could've seen the future, he would have told Beth how she was to make him feel…eventually. He would have, at least, tried to explain how in the future, her soul sings to him every time he thought about the time they spent together. How he now, stole moments of solitude, hiding in hotels with shut terraces and 'Go Away' signs hanging on the doorknobs, hoping to capture some 'passion' again and again. "For tonight, your name is…Beth." He'd tell the girls from the escort service as they'd change into the silk lingerie he bought from the Brazilian Boutique. Iman lived in the passion.

"Make sure she's 5'5, brown eyes, about 144-45 pounds, caramel skin with dimples." His specs were specific because he was trying to create as close to a replica of 'her' as he possibly could. And what he wouldn't give to feel that same passion once more; just one more night…to caress, to hold her in his arms. And he would catch the sea's tears as she cried for her would-be lost lover to another. A real life woman. And he would store them in the clouds until the God empathized, finally, and wanted to shed a tear with him and it would rain all night long. And he would cuddle under the blankets, spooning her. Each second growing and falling more and more in love with her.

"A real woman."

Iman liked the sound of that; quintessence of everything he wanted. A beauty so rare and exquisite that his art, the beach and even

Tyrone's pacifying Deli would have to fight for the second seat in his heart.

"I wonder how she's doing." Iman thinks to himself, as a yellow jaguar honks heavy on the horn alerting him of his swerving.

"They are too many cars in Barbados" he sighs to himself. "I remember the good old days, when de people actually used to walk around with donkey carts." He catches himself quickly and refocuses on the yellow and white lines that marked the street. These are the only things that are keeping him from slipping into visions again. One might say he was insane, but Iman, Iman was as sane as the sanest thing ever.

As the sun was gradually setting, the mixture of orange, gray, and dark blue created lavender or a purple-ish color that seemed impossible to understand, and even more impossible to describe. He'd seen the sun set before… countless times; each time more breathtaking than the last, but then this evening's coolness seemed to contain some unusual kind of mistiness. What was it? Probably, it was the ocean that had dampened the atmosphere and maybe it was about to rain. Like the water therefore lived suspended in the air instead of going up past the sky in its regular evaporative methods. Meteorological Purgatory.

In the few months leading up to these days, Iman was becoming more and more of an absentee individual. He was living his life through the many dreams that he was having: flashbacks from the past. He wondered if he was normal… if other people felt this way. More and more, perhaps subconsciously rather than intentionally, he began distancing himself from reality. A reality though, that had not been really kind to him, but still, a reality that existed. And one that he had to deal with. A reality in which, he had lost everything that meant anything to him. In other words, Iman had nothing that he needed, but at the same time, he seemed to have everything that he wanted. His mother, grandfather…he didn't have them; neither did he have a love for himself, nor a heritage birthed from his loins, but he had a big house, cars, a house full of food, a pocket full of money and his lifelong dream of being a successful artist was realized. Still, Iman was not happy.

Chapter IV

Iman rolls over on his back; hugging his giant pillow tight and pulling it on top of him. Its warmth; cooling his body like, he guesses, a lap dog enjoying the company of its master would. He pushes it down between his legs and he feels his penis grow a little as the pillow brushes against the shaft. His king sized Serta mattress, plush on his body, begged him to stay just five more minutes in the coziness of his bed. Looking up to the ceiling and tapping his temple with his finger, Iman style, he enjoys another blissfully peaceful moment in his life before he goes out to the hustle and bustle of the humidly hot, yet frigidly cold Barbadian Streets where he stands among hundreds of thousands, as a lone soldier. You never really know loneliness like this.

As Iman rises, he looks at his alarm/clock/radio that just a second ago was blasting 'Could you be loved' by Uncle Bob. It is six O' Clock.

Iman sits up on the edge of his bed; his hands folded like they would be, were they praying, and he leans his elbows on his thighs staring down at the white carpeted floor. Wiping his morning face, he begins thinking about the addition that he was to make to the piece. He begins thinking of a name for this piece.

Iman never planned any of his work. He never really made rough sketches or blueprints. He just did it. That was part of the fun… the rush that he got from creating something beautiful out of nothing.

Once, Iman was kidnapped by a group of drug lords, Colombians, who after hearing about his genius forced him to paint their version of the Mona Lisa. She was to be kneeling, by a sink, bible in one hand, cocaine straw in the other. At first, he was afraid for his life like anyone would be, but after the Colombians assured him of his safety, and insisted that he did a few lines himself, Iman warmed up to hosts and they proved not bad entertainers. As Iman painted for them, they conversed. Iman remembers one telling him, *"Mi hermano. ¿Usted ve esta mala cosa entera del hombre que los medios nos retratan como? Ése no es nosotros que usted conoce."* "My brother. You see this whole bad man thing that the media portrays us as? That's not us you know."

Iman closes his eyes, trying to steal a few more minutes of sleep nodding off in a different direction than the one he woke from.

As the water beat from his head onto his shoulders and drips down his back in the bathroom, the pit pit patter of the pellets hitting his smooth skin sounds like rain on a rooftop. Well, maybe not a rooftop, but more like rain on water, the ocean, during a rainstorm.

Iman tries to twist his roots out of the way and manages to keep some water from his long knotties, but the mist dampens his hair and so he reaches out the shower, grabs the shower cap from the doorknob and covers his head.

Iman steps out of the bathroom and sees Maria, his long-time friend, sitting comfortably on his bed. She also helped him with the upkeep of the house.

"Maria! What de bird is dis… girl you almost scared me half to death." Iman is startled by her presence as he didn't expect her to come in till he had left.

"Iman" Maria says with her raw Bajan accent, "I did knoh you for a long time, yes?"

Maria rejoined the workforce and became a day worker after her son was brutally murdered by some bandits when they tried to rob the store that he was guarding. Before that, he had promised her that she wouldn't have to work again. The plan was that he was going to be a big time calypso singer and make it to the top and so the thing about his mother cleaning floors and dusting windows would be a thing of the past. In his eyes, she had worked hard enough.

When her son died, Maria thought she would never make it through the night. And when she did, she found herself crying weeks after, continuously. He was not her only child. She had a daughter...somewhere. Her daughter had run off with a man years ago, as soon as she'd turn eighteen, and Maria never heard from her again. For all she knew, she could be dead.

But her son was all she had.

He was the one who stuck around. He was the one that promised to be there...forever. And he loved her. Of this, she was sure.

In a way, Maria felt betrayed by her son's death. For a month she thought that everything he told her was a lie. And although she still loved him and missed him, the only way she could deal with his passing was to treat him like a prodigal son. Like he was indeed still alive but that he'd left her... like her daughter. And because she looked at it like this, she dealt with the situation better. She was used to desertion. She'd been left before. At her age, she had been stood up and left waiting and wanting more times than anyone else in the world. More men had disappointed her. Maria had, as they say, been around the block and come back, more than once.

The way she looks tells tales of her life.

She stands five foot four, two hundred and ten pounds; a little plump for her height from years of eating Bajan food and exercising little. Her hair, once black is now turning gray. Her eyes are a light hazel; her pupils dilating with the strain of millions and millions of hours of blinking. Opening and closing them. Opening and closing them. Her posture is good, still. She'd been practicing correct, upright walking and sitting. She was a poor-great; a person poor on the economic bracket but great in their mentality. In her childhood, she had Champaign tastes with lime juice pocket. Her lips were faded pink and cracked, though once luscious and bright. They maintained, however, their fullness. Cracked and lined like her lips, wrinkles marked her face like tattoos growing with her and multiplying daily. Her breasts hung low on her body. Gravity and time together are unforgiving. Her stomach also dropped lower, now by her pelvic area and protruding every time she wore pants was as obvious as the fact that she is graying is. Yet she is beautiful; classically. Like an old cane cutter is beautiful. Like a praying mother is beautiful or like an African daughter toting water on her head in a clay vase is beautiful. Or like a black couple making love on a cool summer's night in the moonlight is beautiful...this woman, Maria is stunning!

Something was, about her. The pain that she knew was evident but there was something about this aged black woman that made her look like she was supposed to be a goddess.

Chapter V

Iman met Maria when they were both working at the Hilton hotel. He was a bell boy and Maria was in housekeeping. This was before he sold his first painting and when they realized that they had both lost special people in their lives…for Maria her only son; for Iman, his mother, they connected at once. There was nothing to keep them from connecting, spiritually with each other. It was like there was a mystic force that drew them together. And although is was hard to explain, there was a peace that they both enjoyed in other's company.

What drove Iman to Maria was her 'coolness' her nonchalant and friendly nature. Her ability to smile and hum through the grimiest situations and Maria liked that Iman was ambitious. In some ways, he reminded her of her son. His dreams of being more than just a little island boy.

"Yeah. It's been years… buh what are you doing hay man. You know you cyan handle NUTTIN over here."

Maria sucks her teeth,

"Stupes… Sorry I scared you. But you dun know-I seen dem small tings already so don't bodda yuhself wid all ah dah.

"What's going on babes? Is everything all right?" Iman's face transforms into a more serious stare, trying hard to figure if Maria had a problem. She already knew that anything she needed, she could ask him and he was going to make sure that it was taken care of.

Iman remembers back when he was working at the Hilton. Maria used to bring him lunch every single day when he was a starving artist, using all his money, struggling to repair and renovate his house. The only thing in the world that could remind him of his histry. And no matter how little it was, it was always something and something is always better than nothing. They would sit together, and enjoy some conversation during their short lunch break. Those were the good days. Maria always had Iman's back, and in whatever way Iman could, he would have her back too…forever. What they had was deep. Maybe not like two peas in a pod and neither one could ever replace the other's lost loved one, but at least they had each other to remind them of their deceased, so now that he was doing better, making a little money with his paintings, he looked out for Maria.

"Iman, I been looking after you for a while now…you like a son to me" Maria says, holding Iman's hand as he sits close by her on the bed looking into her eyes.

Iman smiles and looks down on the ground, breaking eye contact for that brief moment… "Yeah, I know."

"Iman, I been observing you lately, moping bout here, dope out, like somebody do something to you. Now, I know you ain't always a real big happy- happy man but I's don't like to see you like this hay man. Now tell Maria what's really bothering you."

Iman breathes in and lets out a deep breath as a sigh.

At first Iman denies it, "Nothing aint wrong with me…"

Maria stops him sternly, "Iman!"

"Maria, tell me. You believe that man finds love or that love finds man?" Iman asks, hoping for an answer.

Maria stops and thinks for a brief moment and then responds,

"See I know something duh bodering you." She giggles, "You biological man-clock ticking."

Iman laughs, "I didn't know men had clocks too."

"You want sumting to foup?" Maria asks, seriously.

"See, why it always gotta be sex?" Iman asked standing and bracing against the closet door, "men like to be held too you know. And sometimes a man jus wanta be love up, you know?" Iman laughs his response bowing his head and Shacking it from side to side. "But I was just asking though,"

"I hear you bossman."

Maria laughs back. Call and response giggles,

"Well. The truth is, Iman, I don't know what to tell you boy. I ain't really a expert pun love. Shoot, I can't even keep a man. Buh…buh sometimes, love does find we right, but most of de time, when you want something in life, you gotta go out and get it…you know? Yuh does cyan always be passive wid it too yuh know. Yuh's gawh be aggressive…assertive." Maria tenses up her hold on Iman's hand, to emphasize her point.

"I feel you."

Maria was trying to feel around for some more of Iman's feelings.

"Nah, I just been feeling really weird lately, you know, like, lonely, you know."

"You don't have to explain to me baby." Maria says, understanding exactly how Iman was feeling, "The bible said it is not good for man to be alone."

"The bible said that?" Iman asks doubtfully,

"Yeah! I could see I gine gawh tek you to church with me jus' now, plus that's where all the nice girls is anyways.

Iman laughs, "Church. Church is for sinners, girl, you know I'm a saint."

"I hear you Saint Iman. Look, just put youself in position to find love, that's all I got to tell you. In fact, I got a nice niece, she's work at de bank…you want she or wah?"

"Nah, Maria, why you? You know I don't like blind dates."

"Come on, it gine be fun" Maria responds quickly.

"We'll see what happens."

People are always trying to play matchmaker with Iman. He wonders to himself if his desperation shows through; if his loneliness could be seen in his face, as he puts on his overalls getting ready for a long, semi fulfilling a day at the office, wherever as an artist, his office is for the day. As he dresses, he smells the bacon mixing with the strong and deep smell of coffee.

He walks into the kitchen and sees Maria just pouring some coffee into a cup right next to a plate with some food in it that literally had his name on it.

"That's for me?" Iman asks with a broad smile on his face

"Eat ye all of it, Saint Iman"

"Wait? Bacon and Eggs yuh rambam…like is my birf-day or whah?"

Iman thinks to himself, "Breakfast." Iman can't remember the last time he had breakfast at breakfast time. Just like Maria to try to bring a smile to his face right when he needed one.

"Maria. Today, is gonna be a good day."

Iman lets out a deep breath in a sigh, picks up his shoes and walks calmly towards the kitchen,

"You didn't have to do this you know." Iman says to Maria

"Look, just eat de foolish food and shut up, do."

He taps the rim of the door, smiles, and goes back to eat his well-prepared meal.

Chapter VI

Iman paints like he is overcome with the art; the passion exudes though every move he makes. Every dash and stroke is perfect. Head tilted to the right side, his left hand is isolated in the air and index finger pointing to the air, he moves his hand in quick, forceful and sharp angles at times; and at other times, slow smooth curves and angelic motions. For Iman, art is an art.

From a critic's perspective, Iman is god. Tourists come to watch him all the time and they all marvel at his work. Iman paints like a dance, and hardly realizes when there is anyone observing him. Even when they call him,

"Sir, the work you do is remarkable…do you sell?" in their foreign accents, Iman just keeps on painting. Sometimes, children stand in awe, staring at the man in the trance and aspire to be that talented someday. Few of the art students from the school sit outside and attempt to paint him as he is painting. Nothing fazes Iman as he focuses on his work though…not even threats of rain as clouds build up above his fifty foot canvas. In the middle of St. Michael, he is as unbothered as if he was in the middle of a cane field and takes the time to romanticize the mural.

As Iman was polishing up just one piece of his fifty foot mural, he glimpses across the street. He never glimpses across the street. He never does anything when he is painting except…paint. But this time, he glimpses across the street and he sees her. Right as she was coming out of her red convertible to go into the mini mart at the gas station… he sees her. She is the most beautiful thing he's ever seen. From where he stood, he could see her in all her splendor, full sculptured bronze skin, radiating, and she was sparkling; like she had been soaking in the fountain of youth for days. And her hair, dripping from the saltwater that she was just swimming in, only added to his suspicions that she was either a mermaid or an angel. She had a golden soul that immediately attracted Iman to her spirit and she had so much soul. She was…like a painting.

She slammed the door, and shook her head in what seemed like slow motion, trying to drip the water out, brushing it back by running her fingers through her it; part of the beauty of her was obviously her hair.

Her smile was so suggestive and although she wasn't smiling with or at

him, he could feel her presence clear across the road.

Soulmates.

The second he saw her, it was as if the earth stopped in its

rotations and the heaven opened up. He could see the beam of light,

undoubtedly, from heaven around her as she walked and there was no one

that could tell him that she wasn't of God.

Iman jumps off the ladder, Shackily, almost falling, and without

thinking twice, runs full speed in the direction of the spot he saw his

'princess' as she exited her car. He has no idea what he was doing and

even worse, what he was going to tell this mystery woman once he saw

her close up and personal. As he gets closer to the junction, right by the

intersection where he's about to cross the street and steps onto the road, a

huge sand truck zooms past him, Shacking the earth and swaying him as it

passes and honking it's horn to alert the dazed pedestrian. Iman jumps

back onto the sidewalk bending his body from side to side, looking to

make sure this 'angel' had not left. The truck passed almost as quickly as it

appeared. Then another, and another.

"WHAT THE HELL B?"

As they pass, Iman could feel his hope creeping away from him like he was losing something. Through the breaks in vehicles; between the couple C.O.W trucks that pass him by, Iman could see her get out of the store, bust open a coca cola, smile, and get back into the car. Iman runs left of the trucks, hoping to get behind the last one and approach this woman... this empress... but alas, as he pulls around and the last of the trucks whiz off, all he sees is a little red bumper to a little red convertible zooming off leaving a dust trail impossible to follow but also too impossible to forget.

Gone with the wind!

Iman can feel the single tear flow from his eye as he clenches his fists and then bring his palms to his face in total disappointment.

As he returns to his mural, his dropped shoulders tell a tale of sorrow.

He murmurs under his breath "Cha den, not even once a nigga cyan catch a foolish break in this world?' Iman slowly walks back to his mural, but to his surprise, he could not paint away his issues like he normally did.

This one needed some time.

He smiles at the couple that stood analyzing his half done work. They didn't even realize he was staring them down.

He was envying them.

Jealousy crept up on him as he covetously grilled the touring, probably on honeymoon, husband and wife.

How come some people in this world get everything and others get nothing? "How could this be fair…God?" Iman was never really into the whole religion thing, but he had some serious questions for this 'God' and he needed answers. "If all men are created equal," he reasoned, "What the hell is the meaning of this?" Iman stops and thinks about what he wanted to say in this, his prayer. "Now, I never been one to complain right, and I've never asked you for nothing," Iman stops and realizing that he is in the open rushes back to his car. Tears begin to flow from his eyes as he focuses upward speaking in whispers, "not saying that I don't appreciate everything you've done for me, thanks, but if you know you don't want me to have…love, stop teasing me." Iman was talking directly to God…something he'd seldom done before.

Iman leans back in his car and falls asleep.

GOIN' 'BROAD

Chapter VII

The wheels of the jet hit the runway creating an unusual falling feeling deep in Iman's stomach. This is one thing that he's never gotten used to. Despite traveling so much, he still had a little fear of flying. The speed and the noise, together with the bounce and the rough and brisk halt was, to Iman, the most uncomfortable part of the journey. On the plane he ate nothing. Part of him was so anxious that he didn't even realize that *Caribbean Beat,* the in-flight magazine, had an article featuring him.

Only weeks ago he had completed the mural at his former school, what would come be his last painting, and he started tying up things, as far as his business and life went in Barbados. He had to leave. He was selling everything and making a clean break for it. He hardly saw it as running away. To him it was the only way to maintain his sanity. He had to relocate to a place that was more understanding of his feelings. There was nothing left for him in Barbados any more. He had always wanted to leave but he told himself that he was staying around for Maria. He couldn't bear to leave her.

After the funeral, Iman signed a check to the funeral parlor for Maria's death expenses and as soon as he left the gravesite, called his agent to announce his decision to leave Barbados. He told him that it was to be viewed as a hiatus. But Iman really had no intentions on coming back. It was time. As he stood at the edge of his driveway looking up to his house, he wondered to himself if he would miss his place and not only that, but he pondered what it would be that he missed most about the place. He knew he would miss his history. But he couldn't let this history consume him. Moment by moment, it was eating away at his mind. He could not let this happen. He had to start over.

When the real estate agent came, Iman was still outside gazing at the house. He had secured a sitting position at the back of the truck with the hood up and he grabbed a stick of gum. He tried to stay away from sugar, but that moment it seemed like such a fitting time- major sweet tooth! As he chewed loudly, the calming repetition of the chewing gum allowed him some thinking time. At times, this made him a little light headed. But for the most part he began to understand the popularity of candy and chocolate.

"How you doing? Uhh… Mr. E-man?" The real estate agent opens the gate, walks in the property and makes his way to Iman for the cordials. He continues, "Thanks for calling us. I understand you wanna sell the place."

"It's I, man, I- Man." Iman corrects him from the mispronunciation. "Yeah I'm leaving the country. In fact, I'll be gone so soon so I'd really appreciate it if we could fast track the process."

"Okay, okay, okay… I understand completely. Well, why don't we go take a look at what's going on."

Iman finishes his chewing gum, breathes in deeply and spits the sticky blob over the gate onto the road, gets up, shuts down the truck's hood and pointing to the house that they stood in front of, directs the real estate agent inside.

"What's your name?"

"Oh I'm sorry…" the agent shuffles around to get his briefcase and papers in one hand and then extends his had to Iman for a handshake… "I'm Ray. Ray Malone at your service sir."

As they walk around the side and back of the house, all gated, the agent interviewed him,

"This is a really nice property. It's a shame you can't take it with you huh."

Iman smirks, "So true man. I'd take it as a carry on, if they let me."

Ray continues, "You said uhh, you were leaving?"

"I was offered a position at a school in England"

"Oh congratulations man!" Ray exclaimed as they passed the pool and pool house.

"Thank you. Thank you very much. Let's go inside, shall we?"

As they enter the back door into the house, Ray looks surprised by the massiveness of the interior of the house.

"Wooow!" he exclaims, "This house is huge" he says, with an amazed expression on his face.

"Yeah it's big." Iman confirms the agent's observation.

Iman shows the agent everything; all the good qualities of the house and in many cases stunning him.

"What is a good selling point also is the modernity. I don't suppose that we are going to leave it furnished, are we?" Ray asks, glaring at Iman.

"Well…yes. Everything you see here is going to be sold with the house. She comes as is."

"So you live in all this by yourself?"

Iman doesn't answer him.

After showing the entire house, Iman leads Ray down a flight of stairs to a sort of basement, to the den, where they sit in front of the coffee table. Iman sits the briefcase on the table and begins to remove the contents of the briefcase, most of which is paperwork and contracts to be filled out.

"Chew for you?" Iman smiles, offering Ray a gum.

"No thank you."

"Do you mind?" Iman takes out a stick and puts it in his mouth.

"No… please."

"Would you like something to drink Ray?" Iman asks as he walks over to the liquor cabinet.

Realizing that it was mere courtesy and sensing the nervousness in Iman, Ray opts for a drink.

"Sure nothing too strong though, I'm still on the clock, if you know what I mean."

Iman pours two glasses of something and begins to walk back to his seat.

"Man. This house has been in my family for years. My father, father's father..." Iman stops. "You know how the story goes man. You know. I spent time in other places. Brief visits and prolonged stays in many other countries, but I never lived anywhere else. I know no other shelter than the protection of these four walls."

Ray says nothing. He just sits and sips his drink as Iman speaks on.

"I understand completely… well, we're gonna give you that little push you need to start that new life right. And with the money that you make you could buy a whole new set of walls to shelter and protect you. So what are you asking Iman? Because we I think we can get you a buyer before the end of the week. Of course you know we've gotta do paperwork and what not but we can close the deal…uhhh… "

Iman interrupts him, "Well I had a figure in my head. I was playing around with the thought of four."

"Four sounds reasonable, although I think I can get you four-5 probably five if I push."

"Really?" Iman likes the sound of the extra five hundred thousand to a million dollars and he nods his head in agreement. "All right, so here's what we'll do- I'll liaison with the office and give them contact with my lawyer, now that you've seen the house anything and everything else you can talk through with him."

"Sounds good. Thank you!"

"Thank you for coming. He can also sign anything on my behalf."

Iman reaches up to the overhead compartments and pulls out his carry-on bag and fastens it over his shoulders. Making sure all his documents are in order, he heads for the exit. Nothing was to prepare him for what he about to encounter. Besides working a few years at a hotel, he'd never had a formal job in his life. He never used his degrees; neither the B.A in Art History or the MA in the Philosophy of Art and Aesthetics, yet administrators thought he was the man for this job. Sure he was qualified. He'd gone to college. And he had tremendous experience as a professional artist, which is probably what they were looking for, but with regards to him as a teacher or as a professor, as they like to say, this he too had to see. But he was ready. He had waited long enough to get away for good from his homeland. Not because he no longer liked the country. No, to him Barbados would always be home. But the need for something new and different moved him. The same need that kept him up nights before; this need that he'd spoken to Maria about…Maria.

Iman sighs as he thinks about Maria briefly as he proceeded to immigration. While walking, Iman catches eyes with a young English boy, probably coming home from vacationing in the Caribbean and he opens his eyes- widely bulging out his eyeballs to the youngster. The young man sticks out his tongue and shakes his head and then focuses back on the walk.

Iman smiles.

As Iman walks out into the Arrival Lounge, he looks around. He is expecting someone to be there waiting on him. He has only his travel bag or carry-on and one suitcase, as most of his belongings and everything he needs will be shipped to his new residence…in England.

He looks up and continues to bend his head around peering through the crowd. He didn't even know what he was looking for. He figured that it would probably be someone with a sign that said his name on it. He guessed probably that it would be a white man. He laughs. Among the crowd, nine out of ten people is white. As Iman checks his watch getting impatient and trying to decide whether or not to look for a pay phone and call…someone, he sees someone jetting towards him. Iman's lower lip drops. He can't believe his eyes. It is the same girl with the red convertible from the mini mart at the gas station across the street. A smile comes to his face but then his heart begins to beat.

"How could this be?" he says to himself "It's impossible"... He sees her. She is still the most beautiful thing he's ever seen. From where he stood again, he could see her in all her splendor, full sculptured bronze skin, radiating, and she was sparkling; like she had been soaking in the fountain of youth for days. And her hair! He could imagine it dripping from the saltwater that she was just swimming in, in his mind. Now, he was sure she was an angel. She still had a golden soul that immediately attracted Iman to her spirit and she had so much soul. She was...like a painting and Iman could still feel her presence just like the first time he saw her. Iman looks up to the heavens immediately. A 'converted Christian' now and he can hear something whisper,

"Don't mess this up."

All the seconds it took for her to get to him, Iman stared and waited. She approached.

"Oh my gosh- Sir, are you Mr. ..."

Iman interrupts her, "Yes I am...whoever it is you're looking for, I am that person."

She smiles. It is the most beautiful smile Iman has ever seen. "Are you Mr. Iman Reese?"

"Told you!" Iman laughs

"Thank God!" she exclaims. "I left the name plate thingy at home rushing out here." She sighs and jitters out her words, as talkative as a cheerleader explaining why she didn't have her pom-poms.

"No problem. No problem at all. I leave my name plate thingies at home all the time. And what is your name?"

"Oh I'm sorry, I'm Beth." She replies.

It is at this moment that Iman becomes whole.

Chapter VII.5

Iman sits in the office of the VP of Human Resources.

"Thank you so much for accepting our invitation Mr. Reese." Mr. Daniel Shackes Iman's hand and welcomes him emphatically to England and to the job.

"Please. Just Iman sir. And, the pleasure is all mine."

"Well I'm going to tell you all about the job and what it entails. In fact, you'll be wearing more than one hat, if you accept. There's the official job…the reason you are here, which is for you to be the director of the University's Art Gallery." Mr. Daniel tells Iman all about the job description as art curator. Iman likes what he hears. He smiles as he is told about the job.

Mr. Daniel continues, "I don't know if you know this, we actually have a collection of your work."

Iman is surprised as he never had any art shows or classified any of his work in a 'release' fashion.

Mr. Daniel continues, "As a matter of fact, you have a whole room dedicated to your stuff. I'll show you around soon enough. The other hat that is available for you to wear is Professor of Caribbean Art here at University. The faculty is desperately in need of someone versed in that area and we think that you will fit in perfect."

Iman sits and takes in all that Mr. Daniel, the VP, is saying. Most of him is excited about the opportunity. The fact that he will be starting a new career in a new country. He pulls himself together to begin gathering new experiences. Part of him is nervous, as he does not know what to expect and the other part of him cannot stop thinking about Beth. In fact, most of him that is excited about the job opportunity now focuses on this woman… Beth! What a woman.

His mind drifts off in a world dominated by this vision of rare perfection as Mr. Daniel continues to speak. He appears to be listening but all he can hear is the Charlie Brownish way of speaking as he struggles to concentrate on what the VP is saying. It is difficult.

"Very good! I was told that you were very informal and unconventional but I had no idea. This is a great thing. I think you're going to connect perfectly with the students at this University. They may even be able to identify with you on a level they can't with other professors. Welcome to the job!"

Mr. Daniel rises and extends his hand for a handshake. Iman follows and does the same.

"Thank you!" He replies.

"Listen. If there is anything at all; any way I can be of service, please let me know."

As Iman leaves the office and walks into the hallway, he sighs deeply, letting loose his tie fastened around his neck. He walks outside observing as he walked along the students as they went about their business. He peered through the vast plethora of frenzied college students searching through the crowd to see whether he could discern which or which was not an Art major or Art Philosophy major.

The mere thought of the game made him smile as he pushed the huge double doors leading outside of the Hugh Droggin Administrative Building. As soon as he got outside he adjusted his coat as the weather had cooled since he'd last been outside; winter, something he would need to get used to, and he ripped a stick of gum.

"Those things'll kill you you know."

He heard a voice say. He knew this voice. How could he forget it? It was Beth. He turns around with a huge smile on his face, silently greeting the goddess.

"Have another?"

Iman reaches into his coat pocket, reaches for the pack and turns it towards Beth.

"You have the time?" she asks,

Iman feels around his pocket areas wondering where last he placed his cell phone. He finds it, in time shows it to Beth.

"You're much more mellow than I remember. Is this the same man from the airport?"

Iman smiles, "Well, I am just a little dumbfounded by your beauty...Beth."

"Ahhhhh, you remembered my name." Beth replies, "Very good."

Iman and Beth exchange a few words while loitering, mostly small talk and then Beth turns and mentions that she has to go. As she adjusts her coat, after looking at her watch, Iman stops her-

"Wait Beth, I was wondering if you would, I don't know, like to go to the pub later or a restaurant or something after work." Iman finally makes his move. He feels for a response, completely unaware of the popular or acceptable dating spots among English people. Beth smiles as he fidgets during his approach.

She stalls for a second and then she responds "Sure, I'd like that very much."

"Really?" Iman is ecstatic and Beth can see the joy radiating from his face. "Good. Well, I'll meet you here after work then…about 5.00?"

"Sure, see you later then."

END OF PART I

WITH LOVE!

ABOUT THE AUTHOR

Jeremy Davis is a young writer and a seasoned Nomad who considers himself a citizen of the world.

He has chosen to pursue a career as a socially conscious Writer and Explorer but he also works as a Marketing and Creative Consultant when called upon. Jeremy also enjoys teaching and working with young people.

He is an alumnus of Andrews University, via their extension site in Trinidad and Tobago, and a graduate student at Long Island University.

Jeremy Davis has shared the stage with writers and poets both in the US and the Caribbean including Saul Williams and Tehut Nine in New York, and DJ Simmons, Adrian Green and Kamau Braithwaite in Barbados... among others. He is published and reviewed in newspapers and journals and has also worked as a ghostwriter, editor and creative consultant in places such as Mainland China and Hong Kong, as well as other parts of Asia, Guyana and certain parts of South America, the Caribbean, the United States and Canada. He enjoys the research process associated with international 'gigs'. He has taught and motivated hosting youth writing conferences on 'The Art of Passionate Public Speaking' and 'Developing a Plot', among other themes and topics. He has consulted with businesses on the subject 'How to improve a My Marketability Using Creative Content and Social Media'. He is the author of three books.

When asked why he writes, his answer is simple: "I want to provide people with an escape from their harsh realities, even if it's just until they put down my books." He does not believe that any one genre can truly define him so he has studied them all in an effort to make a more informed decision.

ANNOUNCEMENTS

Call for Submissions

J-Afrikah always considers assisting in the publishing efforts of talented young writers.

Bookings and Speaking Engagements

I speak and headline at:

- Conferences
- Motivational Seminars
- Events and Shows

I also:

- Host Writing Workshops and tutor
- Entertain at Activity Days
- Motivate and work with Special Needs Children and Differently Able'd Individuals

<u>-I believe in inclusive learning-</u>

Inquire about my many Literary and Creative Consulting Services including:

- Writing
- Ghostwriting
- Editing
- Proofreading,

LINKS

http://jafrikah.blogspot.com/

http://www.facebook.com/JAfrikah

https://twitter.com/JAfrikah

http://www.youtube.com/Daddy1021

http://www.linkedin.com/in/jard1021

http://www.amazon.com/author/jafrikah

CONTACT ME

jeremydavisiv@hotmail.com

jeremyd4@gmail.com

I look forward to hearing from you!

Made in the USA
Charleston, SC
17 July 2013